WITHDRAWN

W9-AWN-193

d, 8 42 24 N.   cos, 9.99496   cos, 9.99496   d, 26 22 30 S.   cos, 9.95426   cos,

hav, 9.16310   hav, 8.75141   hav, 8.52542

$L\sim d$, 11 47 54 nat. hav, .14558 $L\sim d$, 23 17 00 nat. hav, .05642 $L\sim d$, 41 49 18 nat. hav, .03353
               nat. hav, .01056   nat. hav, .04072   nat. hav, .12739

z, 46° 33'.0   nat. hav, .15614   cosec, 13908 z, 36° 19'.2   nat. hav, .09714   cosec, 22747 z, 47° 18'.0   nat. hav, .16092   cosec, .13376

h_c 43 27.0   sin, 9.98480 h_c 53 40'.8   sin, Z=S 47° E. (133°) 9.86651 h_c 42 42.0   sin, Z=25°.5 9.63435
h_o 43 30.0   Z=75° h_o 53 41.1 h_o 42 43.8

Int., 3.0 towards 75°   Int., 0.3 towards 133°   Int., 1.8 towards 25°.5

h_c 43° 37'.4 (Tab. 40), −1'.0 h_c 53° 48'.2 (Tab. 40), −0'.7 h_c 42° 51'.3 (Tab. 40), −1'.1
Corr., − 7.4   H.E., −5.4   Corr., − 7.1   H.E., −5.4   Corr., − 7.5   H.E., −5.4
                I.C., −1.0   I.C., −1.0   I.C., −1.0
h_o 43 30.0   Corr., −7.4 h_o 53 41.1   Corr., −7.1 h_o 42 43.8   Corr., −7.5

Fix at 1820 Lat. 3° 04' S., Long. 92° 29' E. "Altair" position line is carried forward 2 miles and "Vega" position line is moved backward 1 mile to bring all position lines to 1820
Run to 2000

Co   Dist.,   D. L.,   Dep.,   D. Lo.,
304°   25'   14'.0   20'.7   20'.7

1820 Pos., Lat., 3° 04' S.   Long., 92° 29' 0 E.   1820, D. R., 3° 05'.5 S.   Long., 92° 27'.8 E.
Run,   D. L., 14 N.   D. Lo., 20.7 W.   Run,   D. L., 14.0 N.   D. Lo., 20.7 W.
2000 Pos., Lat., 2 50 S.   Long., 92° 08.3 E.   2000 D. R., Lat., 2 51.5 S.   Long., 92 07.1 E.

Set=39°
Drift .13 per hour

Behold the Bold Umbrellaphant

and Other Poems

BY Jack Prelutsky   ILLUSTRATIONS BY Carin Berger

PORTER MEMORIAL BRANCH LIBRARY
NEWTON COUNTY LIBRARY SYSTEM
6191 HIGHWAY 212
COVINGTON, GA 30016

Greenwillow Books, *An Imprint of* HarperCollins*Publishers*

To David-Paul and Claire,
Zoe and Hokulani
—J. P.

With love to my loves
—C. B.
(with special thanks to AR)

Behold the Bold Umbrellaphant and Other Poems

Text copyright © 2006 by Jack Prelutsky

Illustrations copyright © 2006 by Carin Berger

All rights reserved. Manufactured in China.

www.harpercollinschildrens.com

Collages were used to prepare the full-color art.

The text type is 18-point Polymer-Medium Roman.

Library of Congress Cataloging-in-Publication Data

Prelutsky, Jack.

Behold the bold umbrellaphant and other poems / by Jack Prelutsky ;

pictures by Carin Berger.

 p. cm.

"Greenwillow Books."

ISBN-10: 0-06-054317-5 (trade bdg.) ISBN-13: 978-0-06-054317-4 (trade bdg.)

ISBN-10: 0-06-054318-3 (lib. bdg.) ISBN-13: 978-0-06-054318-1 (lib. bdg.)

1. Animals, Mythical—Juvenile poetry. 2. Children's poetry, American.

I. Berger, Carin, ill. II. Title.

PS3566.R36B36 2006 811'.54—dc22 2005022185

First Edition 10 9 8 7 6 5 4 3 2

Greenwillow Books

Contents

Behold the Bold Umbrellaphant

Behold the bold UMBRELLAPHANT
That's not the least afraid
To forage in the broiling sun,
For it is in the shade.
The pachyderm's uncanny trunk
Is probably unique,
And ends in an umbrella
That has yet to spring a leak.

And so the bold UMBRELLAPHANT
Is ever at its ease,
No matter if the temperature
Is ninety-nine degrees.
And when a sudden thunderstorm
Sends oceans from the sky,
That fortunate UMBRELLAPHANT
Remains entirely dry.

um-BRELL-uh-fint

The Bizarre Alarmadillos

The bizarre ALARMADILLOS
Are a clamorous quartet,
For they're in a constant frenzy . . .
They're incessantly upset.
You'd imagine they'd be calmer,
No one means them any harm,
And besides, they're thickly armored,
Yet they're always in alarm.

When they push their panic buttons,
Buzzers buzz and beepers beep.
Brass alarms clang ever louder,
It's no wonder they can't sleep.
Then they flail their tails in terror
As they holler and they whoop—
Yes, those four ALARMADILLOS
Are an odd and noisy group.

uh-larm-uh-DILL-owes

The Ballpoint Penguins

The BALLPOINT PENGUINS, black and white,
Do little else but write and write.
Although they've nothing much to say,
They write and write it anyway.

The BALLPOINT PENGUINS do not think,
They simply write with endless ink.
They write of ice, they write of snow,
For that is all they seem to know.

At times, these shy and silent birds
Will verbally express their words.
But mostly they do not recite—
They aim their beaks and write and write.

The Lynx
of Chain

links-of-CHAIN

The sun is up, and on the plain,
We see and hear the LYNX OF CHAIN,
Which, dazzling in the early light,
Is truly a resplendent sight.

As all around the plain it bounds,
It makes resounding clanging sounds,
So as it circumnavigates,
The morning air reverberates.

22 ⑨ 644

2.29

The LYNX OF CHAIN must not forget
To vanish when the weather's wet,
For water soon would make it rust,
Reducing it to orange dust.

It keeps a sharp and watchful eye
On every cloud that happens by.
And that is why the LYNX OF CHAIN
Is never spotted in the rain.

The Pop-up Toadsters

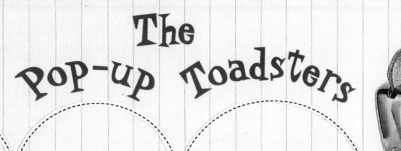

The POP-UP TOADSTERS hop and hop,
Then startlingly, abruptly stop
And place in slots atop their heads
Fresh slices of assorted breads.

A minute passes, two at most,
Then up pop perfect pairs of toast,
Which happily don't go to waste,
For TOASTERNS now arrive in haste.

They snatch the toast up in their beaks,
And soar away with joyful shrieks.
And now, with empty slots on top,
The POP-UP TOADSTERS hop and hop.

POP-up TOWED-sturz

Shoehornets

SHOEHORNETS make it easier
For you to put on shoes.
They quickly slide
Your feet inside.
You can, of course, refuse.

And that is what you'd better do,
For you should know one thing—
It's true they choose
To help with shoes,
But when they do . . . they sting!

shoe-HORN-its

pan-thur-MOM-it-ur

Here Comes a Panthermometer

Here comes a PANTHERMOMETER,
A cat we fondly hail,
For we can tell the temperature
By looking at its tail.
Its tail is clearly accurate,
As we have often found,
And so the PANTHERMOMETER
Is nice to have around.

Here comes a PANTHERMOMETER,
A feline we adore.
It's always set to tell us
What the weather has in store.
It tells us when we're sweltering,
And when we're apt to freeze—
We praise the PANTHERMOMETER
That helps us by degrees.

Page 11

The Circular Sawtoise

The CIRCULAR SAWTOISE does little but yawn,
Until it sees something that needs to be sawn.
And then, with such skill that it merits awards,
Turns trees into logs, which it saws into boards.

The CIRCULAR SAWTOISE may seem to be slow,
But when it is sawing, that's simply not so.
Its shell doesn't hinder its furious pace,
And shields it from chips that might fly in its face.

It saws and it saws, rarely stopping to rest.
It saws with proficiency, fervor, and zest.
At last, when its sawing is done for the day,
The CIRCULAR SAWTOISE just lumbers away.

SIR-cue-lur SAW-tiss

The Limber Bulboa

The limber BULBOA is hard to ignore,
It's out every night, for it loves to explore.
It has no idea what it's likely to find
As it lights up its way with its brilliant behind.

It winds around meadows, meanders by trees,
Shining its light on whatever it sees.
It studies the land as it wanders about,
Its light is amazing, and never goes out.

It's wondrous to watch the BULBOA behave,
It turns up its beam when it peers in a cave.
It lights up the sands as it winds down the shore—
The limber BULBOA is hard to ignore.

bulb-OWE-uh

The Clocktopus

CLOCK-tuh-puss

Emerging from the salty sea,
A wondrous beast appears.
It clearly is a CLOCKTOPUS,
We marvel as it nears.
It moves with slow precision
At a never-changing pace,
Its tentacles in tempo
With the clock upon its face.

While undulating east to west
Across the swirling sand,
It ticks away the minutes,
And it has a second hand.
We watch it for an hour
And it never goes astray—
There's nothing like a CLOCKTOPUS
To tell the time of day.

The Eggbeaturkey

The EGGBEATURKEY's whisklike legs
Are excellent for beating eggs.
They beat them by the dozen, then
They often beat those eggs again.

They beat them to a foamy froth,
Which, stirred into a hearty broth,
Is so delicious that we cheer—
We're glad the EGGBEATURKEY's here.

egg-bee-TUR-key

hatch-ICK-inz

Hatchickens

HATCHICKENS are odd,
And the reason is that
Instead of a head,
They have only a hat.
They muddle about
In a permanent daze,
In bowlers and beanies,
Sombreros, berets.

HATCHICKENS are truly
Ridiculous fowls . . .
They strut and they swagger
In kerchiefs and cowls,
In turbans and derbies,
In bonnets and caps,
Fedoras and fezzes,
And helmets with straps.

Because they can't hear,
And because they can't see,
They bump one another
Continually.
Of course they can't eat,
And they can't even cluck—
Those hapless HATCHICKENS
Are lacking in luck.

The Trumpetoos and Tubaboons

(Fig. 36)

trum-pet-OOZE

The TRUMPETOOS and TUBABOONS
Are blaring out discordant tunes.
They play them loud, they play them long,
But most of all, they play them wrong.

They open up their brazen throats,
Unleashing a barrage of notes
That would be better left unplayed . . .
But play they do as they parade.

too-buh-BOONS

8051

W.R.D
13.3.13
Y.A.

Their sounds are jarring to the ear,
As noisily they persevere
And play in clashing beats and keys
Unmusical cacophonies.

They march about in close array.
We wish they'd simply march away,
Or stop and take a silent snooze—
Those TUBABOONS and TRUMPETOOS.

(Fig. 35, *f*)

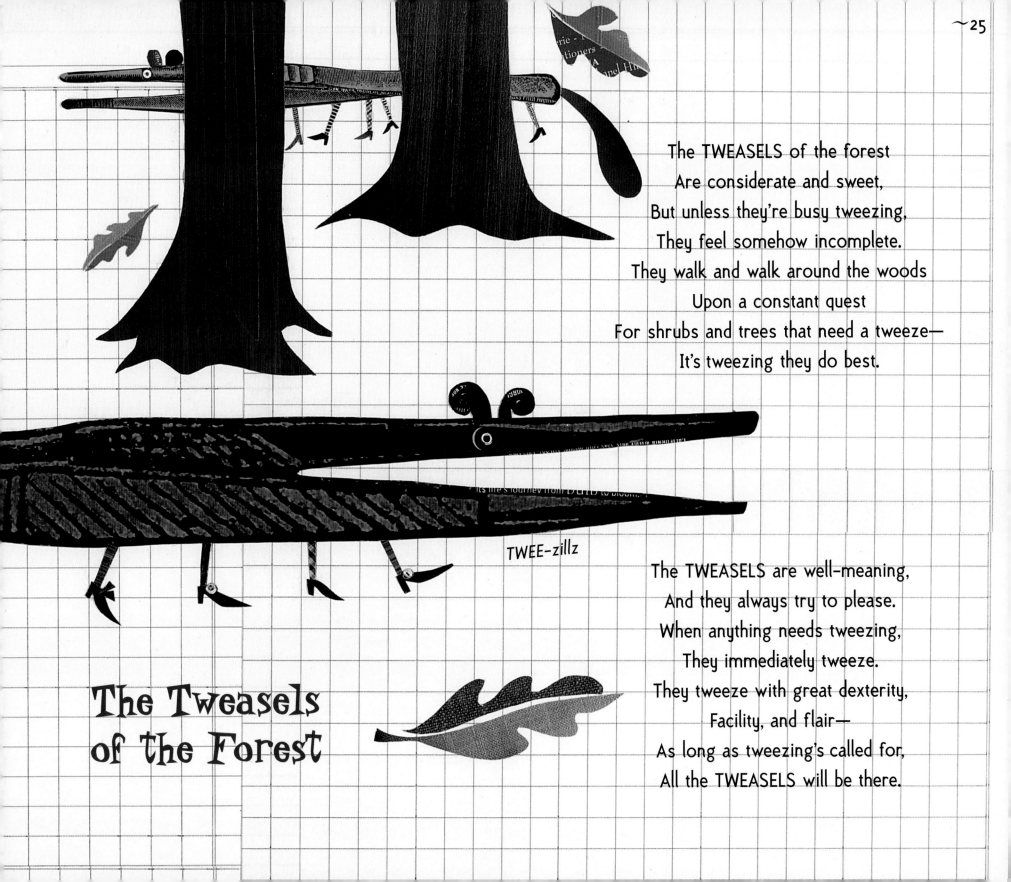

The TWEASELS of the forest
Are considerate and sweet,
But unless they're busy tweezing,
They feel somehow incomplete.
They walk and walk around the woods
Upon a constant quest
For shrubs and trees that need a tweeze—
It's tweezing they do best.

TWEE-zillz

The TWEASELS are well-meaning,
And they always try to please.
When anything needs tweezing,
They immediately tweeze.
They tweeze with great dexterity,
Facility, and flair—
As long as tweezing's called for,
All the TWEASELS will be there.

The Tweasels
of the Forest

The Tearful Zipperpotamuses

The tearful ZIPPERPOTAMUSES
Regularly cry.
They seldom cease their weeping,
And they seldom even try.
They have zippers on their bellies,
On their legs and heads and backs,
But their zippers keep unzipping,
So they rarely can relax.

The dreary ZIPPERPOTAMUSES
Stand around and mope. . . .
If all their zippers opened
They would surely have no hope.
Their zippers help contain them,
So they worry and they fret
That their insides will fall outside,
Though this hasn't happened yet.

Those fearful ZIPPERPOTAMUSES
Find it very hard
To keep their zippers zippered,
So they're constantly on guard.
Perhaps they wouldn't spend their days
With such a sense of dread,
If they took out all those zippers
And put buttons in instead.

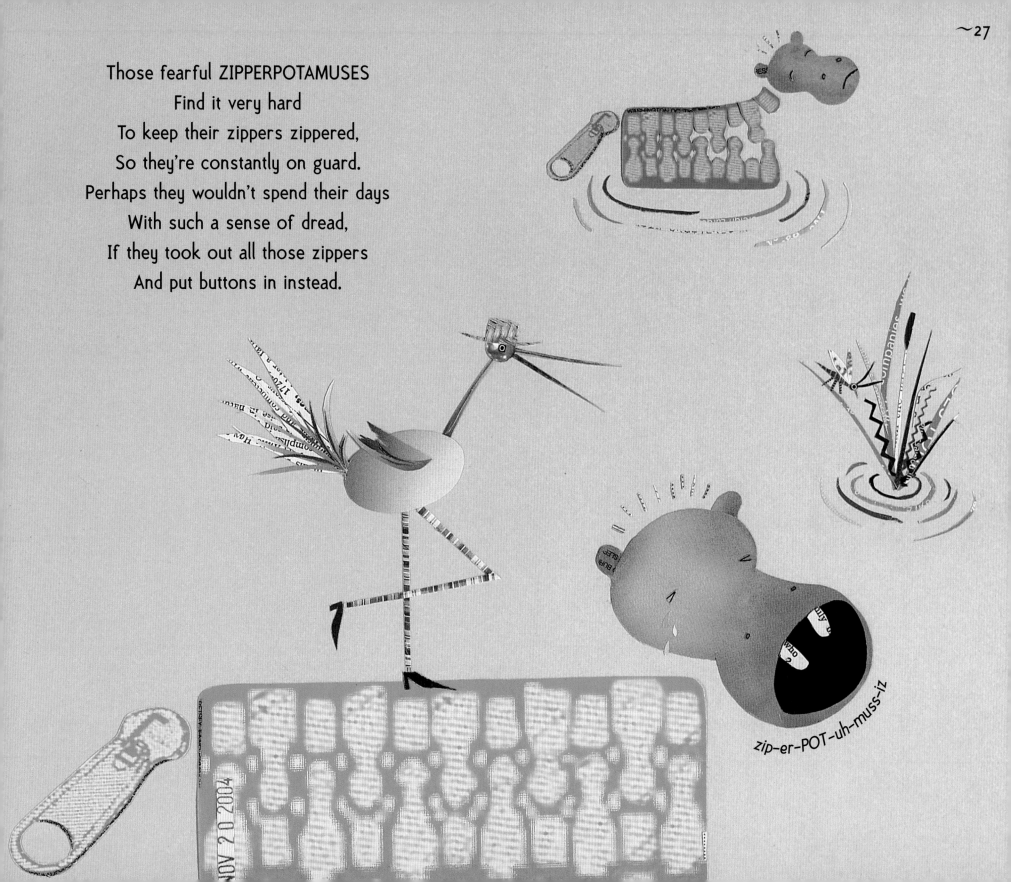

zip-er-POT-uh-muss-iz

The Ocelock

OSS–ih–lock

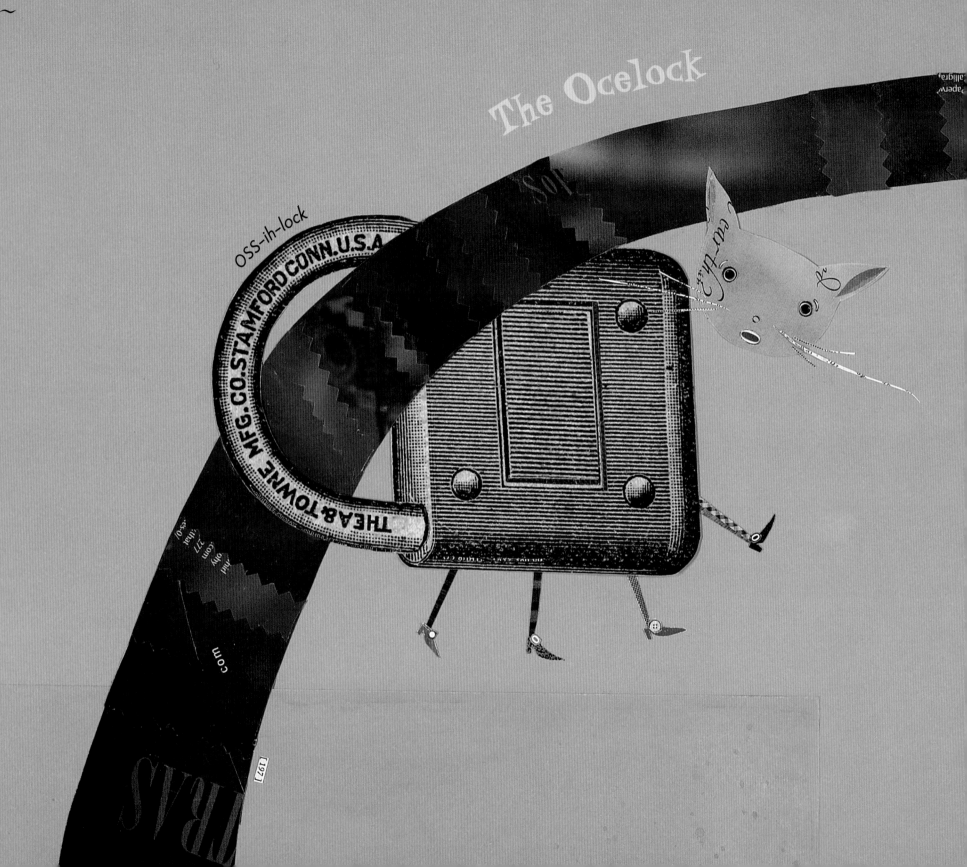

KEY-mun-key

The OCELOCK is out of luck.
It cannot move, it's simply stuck.
It's waiting for a KEYMONKEY
To open it and set it free.

By accident, apparently,
It locked itself around a tree.
No wonder that it seems in shock—
We're sorry for the OCELOCK.

The Solitary Spatuloon

At home within a blue lagoon,
The solitary SPATULOON
Calls longingly as it glides by—
"Syrup!" is its plaintive cry.
The fowl, both curious and rare,
Now flips a pancake in the air.
Its tail, we note, is well designed
With this peculiar task in mind.

We watch with wonder and delight,
Until it vanishes from sight.
Yet, even as it disappears,
Faint strains of "Syrup!" fill our ears.
We wait, and as we wait we yearn,
In hopes the bird will soon return.
But sadly, in the blue lagoon,
We fail to spy the SPATULOON.

spat-chew-LOON

BIBLI

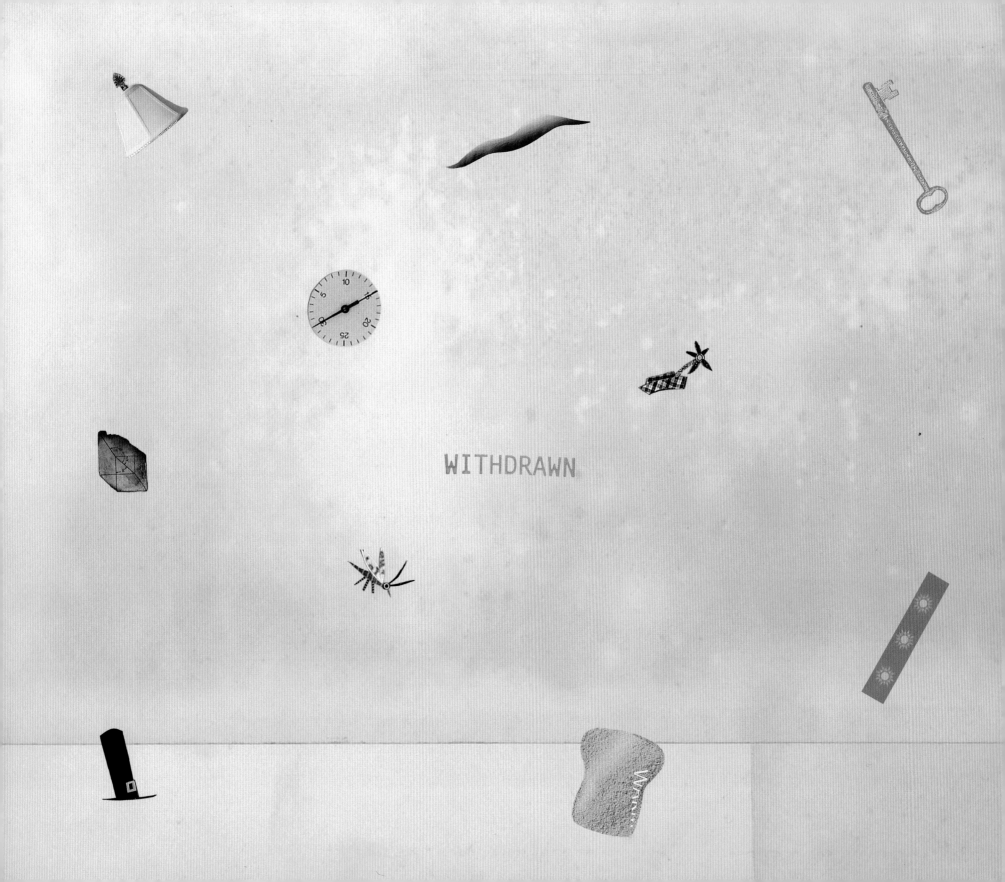

WITHDRAWN